The Junior Novelization

TinkerBell
AND THE
LOST TREASURE

The Junior Novelization

Adapted by Kimberly Morris

Random House 🏠 New York

Chapter One

Lyria, the best storytelling fairy in Pixie Hollow, hovered in front of an elaborate tapestry. She was searching for inspiration for a new poem—a poem she would recite at the Autumn Revelry.

The tapestry depicted the nature fairies: the special group of fairies who changed the seasons four times a year on the mainland. Right now, Lyria knew, those special fairies were making sure that autumn arrived in all its splendid glory.

Words began to come to Lyria as she stared at the wondrous tapestry. She recited them quietly, her eyes lingering on the dazzling colors of fall.

"The changing of the seasons
Brings wonder to the world.
For ages has the magic
Of the fairies been unfurled.
But nature's greatest changes
Come beneath the autumn sky.
And mysteries reveal themselves
As harvest time draws nigh.
This year, a shimmering blue moon
Will rise before the frost.
Perhaps its rays can light the way
To find what has been lost."

Lyria closed her eyes and pictured what was happening on the mainland. She imagined the teams of fast-flying fairies that glided over the trees, trailing pixie dust behind them. Magically, green leaves turned yellow, orange, and red in their wake.

In a sunflower patch, garden fairies stripped tattered petals from their stalks. Waiting birds with woven baskets hurried to catch the falling sunflower seeds. The fairies would bring the seeds back to Pixie Hollow to be stored until next spring, when they would change the season again.

Vidia, the fastest of the fast-flying fairies, spun through the woods, creating whirlwinds that sent leaves flying off the trees and floating through the air.

Beck, an animal fairy, darted from tree to cave, tucking in the hibernating creatures for their long nap after making sure each one had eaten a large and nourishing meal.

Fawn, another animal fairy, took charge of the migrating creatures. She led a group of geese down a long runway. She gave them the signal to take off and then dove forward just in time to avoid being run over by the V-shaped flock.

Oh, if only humans could see how busy the fairies were! But they never did. And they never would. All they would know was that one day, miraculously and seemingly overnight, autumn had arrived.

By then, the fairies who had worked so hard to make it happen would already be speeding toward the Second Star to the Right, hurrying home to Pixie Hollow to celebrate the completion of their work at the Autumn Revelry.

Back in Pixie Hollow, the dust-keeper fairy Terence zoomed back toward the Dust Distribution Depot at top speed. There was a lot to do! So many fairies and supplies had to be flown back and forth from the mainland that it seemed as if he just raced from one dust delivery to the next.

It was pixie dust that kept everybody and everything in the air. So during a season change, the dust-keeper fairies worked day and night. And the rules were strictly enforced: One teacup of dust per fairy per day. No more. No less. Every particle was precious.

Terence flew into the bustling depot where the pixie dust was prepared for distribution. He landed next to his friend Stone, who was standing on the production line. "Good morning, Stone."

"Hey, Terence," Stone answered, glad to see his buddy.

The two friends tossed bags back and forth like jugglers before depositing them neatly on the conveyor belt.

Before they could resume their game, Fairy Gary came marching through, barking orders at the top of his voice. "Come on! Let's go! Flap your wings! Those fairies on the mainland won't be able to fly home without pixie dust. Terence, have you delivered the pixie dust rations to the scouts yet?"

"Yes," Terence answered. "I just finished today's."

"Remember," Fairy Gary said, "one cup each. No more. No less."

Terence nodded. "I know, Fairy Gary."

On the other side of the depot, the timekeeper pulled a lever that sent a sleeping beetle into a flower amplifier. The startled beetle awoke with a loud *BZZZZZZZZZ*, signaling that the shift was over.

Terence prepared to fly away.

"Where are you off to?" Fairy Gary asked as he smiled slyly at Bolt and Flint, two other dust-keepers.

"Oh . . . just doing some errands and stuff," Terence answered evasively.

Bolt gave Flint a knowing wink. "Errands, eh?"

"And *stuff*," Flint reminded Bolt.

Terence knew they were teasing him about his friend Tinker Bell. But sometimes it was just better to play dumb. "Why are you guys talking like that?"

Flint and Bolt grinned and answered as one. "Nooooo reeeeeeason."

"Say hi to Tinker Bell," said Fairy Gary with a smile.

Terence flew away, determined to ignore their teasing and make a dignified exit. Unfortunately— *BLAM! BANG! BOING!*—he flew straight into a shelf full of pots.

The other dust-keepers laughed when Terence emerged from the mess with a rubber band around his neck. Even Terence couldn't help laughing. He removed the rubber band. "Is it okay if I take this?"

Fairy Gary grinned. "Sure."

"Thanks. See you tomorrow." Terence took off, heading for Havendish Stream, where Tinker Bell was working on a new boat.

Tinker Bell was brilliant. She was imaginative.

She was stubborn. Sometimes she was just plain crazy.

Being around Tinker Bell isn't always easy, Terence thought with a smile, *but it's always interesting.* Because with Tinker Bell, you never knew what was going to happen next.

Chapter Two

Tinker Bell's projects were so exciting that her friends always wanted to help, whether she wanted them to or not. Today, Tink had two assistants working on the boat project: Cheese, an extremely helpful mouse, and Flutter, a not-so-helpful bird.

Flutter meant well, but he kept accidentally dropping hammers near Tinker Bell's head.

The boat, which was made of a hollowed-out gourd, sat perched on a ramp. Tink quickly slid underneath the boat to check the paddle wheel.

"Try it now, Cheese."

Cheese pedaled, and the paddle began to turn.

"That's it. Keep going. Keep going."

"Special delivery for Tinker Bell," called out a familiar voice.

Tink scooted out from beneath the boat. It was Terence!

"Hey! Who's your best friend that always delivers?" he asked.

"Iridessa!" Tink answered promptly.

"Nope. Try again."

Tink cocked her head and pretended to think hard. "Fawn?"

"Me!" Terence said, his face falling.

Tink grinned so that Terence would know she had been teasing all along. "Just kidding!" She gestured to her boat. "What do you think about the *Pixie Dust Express*?"

"The guys are going to love this back at the depot. Sure is going to help out on the river outpost deliveries."

"What's that stretchy thingy?" Tink pointed to the rubber band Terence was holding.

Terence handed it to her. "I thought you could use it for your motor."

Tinker Bell took the rubber band and stretched it . . . and stretched it . . . and stretched it until— *SNAP!*—it pulled itself back into shape and sent Tink spinning into a tangled twist.

Tink was impressed with the force and the speed. "I think it's going to be perfect."

Tink and Terence wound the rubber band tighter and tighter around the paddle wheel. Flutter and a bee brought a twig clip to hold it in place.

Tink hopped into the boat and took the wheel. "All right, Cheese. Ready to launch?"

Cheese released the brake, and the boat slid gently into the water.

"It floats!" Tink cried happily.

Cheese, Flutter, and the bee all made chirping, buzzing, and cheering sounds. Terence quickly fashioned a leaf into a kayak and paddled beside Tink. "Ready for the official test run? Don't worry, I'll be right next to you. All set?"

Tinker Bell nodded. "Check," she replied eagerly.

"Let 'er rip," Terence said.

Tink pulled the rip cord and the boat took off,

kicking up a huge wave that washed over Terence and his leaf kayak. Terence swallowed a mouthful of water and sputtered as his boat began to sink lower and lower.

Tink hoped Terence could stay above water long enough to see what a masterpiece of engineering her boat was. Talk about fully loaded—this baby had options galore. "And now for the hydro-drive," she shouted.

Tink pulled another lever made of a twig.

THWACK! THWACK!

Wings made of bark unfolded from the sides of the boat, and skis popped out of the bottom.

Tink loosened the rubber band, and the paddle wheel began to spin like a fan. Her gourd boat went faster than she had dreamed possible.

Maybe a little too fast.

A bug came flying toward Tink's face. She ducked just in time. The bug flew past her, but when she turned, she saw it fly right into Terence's mouth. "Arghghghgh!" he cried as he spit the bug out.

Tink whipped her head around to face forward again. Her eyes widened. *Oh, no!* The boat was approaching the other side of the river!

KERACK! KERACK!

The skis snapped off as the gourd went skidding up the bank, gaining even more speed.

"Yeeeeowww!" Tinker Bell yelled.

But the boat kept going . . . going . . . going . . . heading straight for a tree!

Tinker Bell closed her eyes and waited for the crash.

But instead of crashing, the boat kept moving, buzzing its way up the tree's trunk until, slowly but surely, it ground to a halt in the uppermost branches.

Tink opened her eyes. She couldn't believe it. This was amazing! Astounding! A miracle! Not only was she still alive, but the boat was in one piece. A little tinkering, a little fixing, and everything would be just fine.

Well, everything would have been fine . . . if it just hadn't been for that darned gravity thing.

CREEEEEAK!

The weight of the boat was too much for the slender branches on which it was perched.

Uh-oh!

The last thing Tink saw was the amazed stare of

a red-headed woodpecker as she tumbled past him.

"Aiiiiiiiieeeeee!" she shrieked.

Terence had seen the whole thing. He paddled his leaf kayak to the other side of the river and jumped out, hurrying toward the tree Tink had crashed into. "Tink? Tink!" he shouted.

He found her lying on the ground surrounded by broken pieces of gourd, her shattered paddle wheel, and scattered twigs.

"Are you okay?" He gingerly helped her up.

"I'm good," she said, struggling to her feet. "But I guess your delivery guys are going to have to wait a little longer."

Tink sounded very calm and professional. Terence was relieved. He knew she often had a tough time controlling her temper.

Terence studied what was left of the boat. "Wow,

Tink. I'm impressed. Usually when one of your inventions doesn't work out, you overreact. And that's putting it mildly. But you're taking this pretty well. I really admire your self-control."

That was when Terence turned and saw that Tink wasn't taking it well at all. She was actually doing a very dramatic rage dance, making angry faces and kicking her feet behind his back.

Terence sighed. "Never mind."

"I DROVE IT INTO A TREE!" Tinker Bell exploded, unable to contain herself any longer. "Jingles! I can't believe the boat broke. I made it for you."

Tinker Bell sat on the ground, folded her arms over her chest, and pouted.

Terence sat down with his back to hers. He hated for Tink to be unhappy. "It just needs a little tinkering. Who do I know who's a good tinkerer? Let's see. Bobble's a good tinkerer. Fairy Mary's got a lot of experience. Hey, how about Clank?"

Tinker Bell's sense of humor kicked in and she began to laugh.

Before either one could say another word, a blast from a reed kazoo split the air. Only one kind of fairy used a kazoo like that. The summoning fairies were Queen Clarion's helpers. When they showed up, it meant the queen had an urgent need to speak with someone. Alarmed, Terence and Tink looked to the sky and saw Queen Clarion's head summoning fairy, Viola, approaching at top speed. She looked like a fairy on a mission. "Uh-oh!" Terence said. "Someone's in trouble." He looked at Tink.

"I haven't done anything," she insisted. "At least, not lately."

"The stinkbug incident?" Terence asked gently.

Tinker Bell bit her lip. "Ohhhhhh, yeahhh."

Viola swooped down to the ground. "Tinker Bell," she announced, "Queen Clarion awaits."

The expression on Tinker Bell's face was a mixture of defiance, fear, and guilt. Terence hoped whatever trouble she was in this time wasn't too severe. But whatever happened next, he would be there for her. That was what friends were for.

Chapter Three

"It's all a big misunderstanding. I'm sure the queen wants to see me about something completely unrelated," Tinker Bell babbled nervously as she followed Viola to the Pixie Dust Tree.

Viola silenced her with an imperious toot on her kazoo. She pointed to the spot where she wanted Tinker Bell to wait. Viola gave Tink one last, dampening look and flew up the trunk of the hollow tree to announce Tinker Bell's presence to the queen.

As soon as Viola was out of sight, Tinker Bell ducked into the trunk and strained to listen to what was being said in the queen's chambers.

She could hear Queen Clarion's low, melodic voice, and the voice of Fairy Mary, the head tinker fairy. There was also a third voice. A male voice. Who was that?

"Fairy Mary, are you certain?" the voice asked.

"Whatever do you mean?" Fairy Mary replied.

"Only that Tinker Bell, while undoubtedly talented, is also . . ." The voice trailed off.

Fairy Mary finished his sentence. "A hothead? Flies off the handle?"

"Yes," the male voice agreed.

Tinker Bell gulped. She was definitely in trouble. She just wasn't sure with whom.

Fairy Mary continued. "I believe she deserves a chance, Minister."

Minister? Tinker Bell gasped. Now she recognized the voice. It was the Minister of Autumn!

Oh, no! Was he mad at her, too? Who knew he cared so much about stinkbugs?

"After all," Fairy Mary went on, "tinker fairies learn from their mistakes."

"Very well," the Minister of Autumn finally agreed.

"Tinker Bell!" Queen Clarion called out, summoning Tink up the trunk to her chambers.

Tinker Bell took a deep breath. It sounded as if Fairy Mary was prepared to stick up for her. That was good. If she was in trouble with both the queen *and* the Minister of Autumn, she was going to need a lot of help.

Tinker Bell was already talking quickly and apologetically when she flew into the queen's chambers. "It's not my fault, Your Highness. Those stinkbugs were asking for it."

There was a long pause while Queen Clarion, the Minister of Autumn, and Fairy Mary looked at her in confusion. Queen Clarion's graceful eyebrows rose in surprise. The Minister of Autumn looked puzzled. And Fairy Mary smacked her forehead, indicating to Tinker Bell that she had—once again—put her foot in her mouth.

Tinker Bell looked around. Her face began to turn red with embarrassment. "This isn't about the stinkbugs, is it?"

The corners of Queen Clarion's mouth twitched

as she tried hard not to laugh. "No."

"But we can certainly come back to that later," Fairy Mary added in an ominous tone.

Queen Clarion gestured to the tall sparrow man dressed in beautiful gold, orange, brown, and dark green robes. "You do know the Minister of Autumn?"

Tink felt a wave of shyness wash over her. The Ministers of the Seasons were the most important fairies in Never Land, next to the queen.

The Minister's smile was reserved, but his eyes were kind. "Are you familiar with the great Autumn Revelry?"

Tinker Bell grinned. "Well, sure. Everyone's talking about it. They're so excited."

The Minister gestured for her to follow him. He paused outside a large pair of oak doors.

"Since time immemorial, fairies have celebrated the end of autumn with a revelry. And this particular autumn's coincides with a *blue harvest moon*!"

His eyes met Tinker Bell's and held their gaze. "A new scepter must be created to celebrate the occasion." He threw open the oak doors and Tink let out a gasp. "Behold . . . the Hall of Scepters."

It was incredible. Simply incredible.

Tinker Bell stepped through the doors, her eyes trying to take in everything at once. An eerie light filled the hall, where a collection of scepters was on display.

"Every scepter is unique. Some are the work of animal fairies, some of light fairies, or water fairies, or garden fairies. This year, it is the turn of the tinker fairies."

Tinker Bell felt her heart begin to pound.

"And Fairy Mary has recommended you!" he finished.

This was unbelievable. The most amazing thing Tink could ever have imagined. "Me!" she finally managed to gasp. "But . . . but . . . I'm . . . I'm—" She struggled for words. After all, she was still relatively new to Pixie Hollow, and still prone to making mistakes.

"—a very talented fairy," Fairy Mary finished. She gave Tinker Bell a brisk nod of assurance.

"The scepter must be built to precise dimensions. At the top, you will place the moonstone." The Minister led Tink to an ancient tapestry and pointed to the depiction of the Autumn Revelry under a full blue harvest moon. In the tapestry, moonbeams passed through a round gem and emerged as blue pixie dust.

"When the blue moon is at its peak," the Minister explained, "its rays will pass through the gem, creating blue pixie dust."

Queen Clarion took up the tale. "The blue pixie dust restores the Pixie Dust Tree. Like autumn itself, it signals rebirth and rejuvenation. We are relying on you," the queen said to Tinker Bell in a soft but commanding voice.

In the center of the chamber, a large case sat on a table. Fairy Mary opened it and they all gazed upon a gleaming blue stone carefully cushioned on a pillow. "Here is the moonstone," Fairy Mary said. "It has been handed down from generation to generation. Be careful. It is *ridiculously* fragile."

Tinker Bell could see her reflection in the gleaming, glowing surface of the precious stone.

"F-F-Fairy Mary," she stuttered. "I don't know what to say. Thank you." Tink threw her arms around the head tinker and accidentally bumped the pillow. The moonstone wobbled and began to roll.

Fairy Mary reached out to catch it. "Tinker Bell,

you have to be careful!" she cried. Then she closed her eyes and muttered, "One, two, three, four, five, six, seven, eight, nine, ten."

"What are you counting?" Tinker Bell asked.

"It's supposed to calm me down," Fairy Mary answered between clenched teeth.

"Oh," Tinker Bell whispered, determined not to make any sudden moves or loud noises that might upset Fairy Mary.

Fairy Mary returned the stone to its cushioned case and carefully handed it to Tink.

"Don't worry, Fairy Mary. I'll make you proud. All of you." Tinker Bell bowed with great dignity to the queen and the Minister. Then she straightened her back and squared her shoulders, walking out of the room with all the poise she could muster.

Tink strode purposefully out of the hallway, through the queen's chambers. As soon as she was out of sight, she let out a loud "Yahoo!"

Chapter Four

Back in her own little house, Tinker Bell hardly noticed the cheerful chirp of the cricket who lived in her clock and announced the passage of time. She was too busy searching through her trunk of odds, ends, doodads, thingamajigs, doohickeys, and decorative baling wire. Her mind raced with different design ideas for the scepter.

Tink was so preoccupied, she didn't even notice when Terence opened the door and came inside.

"So?" he asked, eager to hear about Tink's visit with Queen Clarion.

"Terence, you're never going to believe this. Guess what happened. Go on," she urged. "Guess!"

Terence rubbed his jaw, thinking. "Well, I—"

"I have been picked to make the new Autumn Scepter!" she blurted out. "Me! Me!" She flew straight into the air and turned a gleeful somersault.

Terence stared. "Hey! That means they gave you the moonstone."

Tinker Bell did another happy spin and fluttered back down. "Want to see it?" She hurried to the case and opened it.

The blue reflection immediately lit Terence's face. He whistled softly.

"Not so close," warned Tink. "Don't even breathe on it. It's fragile."

Terence took a respectful step back. "I know all about it. The blue moon only rises in Pixie Hollow every eight years. The trajectory of the beams of light have got to match the curvature of the moonstone at a ninety-degree angle so the light can transmute into pixie dust."

Tinker Bell stared at her friend, impressed.

"Wow, Terence. How did you know all that?"

"Oh, you know. Every dust-keeper has to study dustology." He grinned, excited now. "You know what this calls for?"

Tink knew where he was going. They had made tea together so many times, they had it down to a dance *and* a science.

Tink got out the tea maker. "Two cups of—"

Terence placed the cups carefully on the counter. "—chamomile tea."

"With extra honey," Tinker Bell added, giving each cup a squirt.

"And some milkweed whip," said Terence.

The hot water, tea, honey, and whip all swirled together to create the perfect beverage.

Tinker Bell and Terence clinked their cups together and each took a sip, savoring not just the tea, but also their friendship and their ability to work in harmony.

"By the way," Terence said. "That new bucket-and-pulley system you made? Fairy Gary loves it."

"Awwww," Tink said modestly. "He's so cute."

"If you say so," Terence said, making it clear that he didn't think Fairy Gary was particularly appealing. He took a thoughtful sip. "You know what? Maybe I can help you. I'm kind of an expert on this. I can collect the supplies. Give you advice."

Tink took a sip of her own tea. "You will? That's so sweet."

"Hey, what are friends for? So what do you say? Can I be your wingman?"

"That would be great. To the best dust-keeper fairy . . ."

". . . and the best tinker fairy." Terence lifted his cup in a toast. "This is going to be a revelry to remember."

"Knock, knock! Good morning!"

The next day, Tinker Bell opened her eyes to see Terence coming through the door at the very moment her cricket clock chirped to wake her. *Wow! Terence sure is punctual,* she thought. This was their first day to work together on the scepter.

Tinker Bell yawned and stretched.

Terence pointed at the calendar on the wall. "All right!" he said in a brisk, up-and-at-'em voice. "We have one full moon until the Autumn Revelry." He picked up a leaf pen and made a big check mark on the calendar.

He darted out the door and was back in a flash with an armful of materials. "I brought you some stuff from work. Maybe there is something here you can use." He dumped the materials next to her workbench.

Tink pawed through the items. Some of it was interesting. Some of it . . . not so much. Still, she was amazed at the number of different things Terence had collected. She picked up a piece of metal and placed it in the fireplace, where the flames would soften it.

Then she turned back to her friend. "Terence, how did you . . ." Her words trailed off. Terence had picked up a spring and was entertaining himself by pressing it against the side of his head.

Tink couldn't help being gratified that Terence was taking such a keen interest. It took a special fairy to appreciate what a miracle of *boiiinng* engineering a spring was. "I can tell you're going to be a big help," she said with a smile.

And he was. All during the day, they worked on the scepter the same way they had made the tea—in perfect harmony.

"Looks good," Terence said as he checked out Tink's latest sketch. "Now remember, you get the most blue pixie dust if you maximize the moonstone's exposed surface area."

Tinker Bell nodded. "Right. Got it."

They went over to the fireplace. Tink turned the softening metal over while Terence skillfully added more logs.

They smiled at each other.

They *were* a good team.

Chapter Five

Day after day, Tinker Bell worked. Time was growing short. The month was flying by. The moon was more than half full, and she was beginning to get nervous.

Tinker Bell had sketched design after design, but Terence always had some opinion about ways to improve the scepter, or some suggestion for changing her approach.

It was nice having help. But the help was starting

to be, well . . . not so helpful. She felt guilty about thinking that way—but she couldn't avoid it. Every day, Terence arrived at the crack of dawn with muffins and advice. The muffins were great, but the constant advice was beginning to sound more like constant criticism. And the "help" seemed more like meddling.

The result was that, after days and days of work, Tinker Bell was behind. Way behind.

The cricket chirped and Tinker Bell sat up in bed, her stomach sinking as Terence came sailing in, punctual as always. "Knock knickity knock. Out of bed, sleepyhead."

Tink flung back the covers and flew to the fireplace to put a piece of metal in. Before she could even position it, Terence was beside her, stoking the fire with a bellows. "You've got to keep the fire nice and hot," he told her (which he really didn't need to, because if anybody knew that a fire had to be nice and hot, it was Tinker Bell).

Terence gave the fire another puff with the bellows. The flames began to smoke and the fire belched a big black cloud.

Tink coughed. She was covered in soot. She bit

back her angry words. After all, Terence was only trying to help.

Tink gritted her teeth and flew to her workbench, rubbing the sleep from her eyes and shaking off the soot. She needed every second to complete her task. She could eat breakfast later.

She picked up the scepter. The base was looking good. The ornate decorations were delicate but not too fussy. While she studied it, planning her next move, Terence came up behind her with a broom, forcing her to move while he swept.

Tink cleared her throat and made a great show of being preoccupied. But Terence didn't take the hint. He continued to sweep around her—here, there, under her feet, under her elbow. She tried to avoid him by moving, but he just followed her wherever she went.

"Excuse me, Tink. You should really try to keep that work space clean. Let me just get that little bit right . . . there!"

Tink let out a loud sigh and moved to the end of her bench.

"Just one more . . . and . . ."

Tink sighed yet again. She moved even more

and—*"ARGHGHGH!"*—fell right off the bench.

Terence looked down at her in surprise. "Whoa!"

Tinker Bell gritted her teeth. She tried Fairy Mary's calming trick. "One, two, three, four . . ."

"Why are you counting?" Terence asked. Then, without waiting for an answer, he turned and continued sweeping.

Tink knew she had had just about all the help she could stand. But when she looked at the calendar, she swallowed her anger. Only a few days left. Only a few. She could do it. She could finish. All she had to do was concentrate and get it done in *spite* of Terence's help.

Over the next few days, Tinker Bell kept her irritation and anger at bay, determined not to let Terence know that he was driving her absolutely, positively crazy. By the end of the week, she was almost finished with the scepter.

Tinker Bell was very proud of herself. She had never worked so hard on anything in her life. Not on the scepter—or on controlling her temper.

Terence hovered, peering over her shoulder. "Watch your angle there," he cautioned. It was all Tink could do not to scream.

Terence picked up a broom and began to sweep, whistling while he worked. The shrill whistle and scratching sound of the bristles were about to drive her mad. How did he think she could get anything done? Still, he was her friend. And . . . he was trying to help.

Tinker Bell held the scepter in her hand. It was almost finished. It was a masterpiece of elegant curves and graceful lines. She wanted to make sure it was finished well before the revelry so that Fairy Mary, Queen Clarion, and the Minister of Autumn could inspect it. Tink wanted it to be one hundred percent perfect.

Terence buzzed around—sweeping, tidying up, and driving Tink nuts. But right now, she refused to let herself be distracted. It was time to add the last and most important touch of all—the moonstone.

Tink opened the case containing the fragile gem.

Just then, Terence picked up the bellows and began pumping the fire. *SQUEAK! SQUEAK!*

Tink carefully lifted the moonstone and held it poised over the tip of the scepter.

SQUEAK! SQUEAK!

"Careful," Terence said as he watched her work.

His interruption broke her concentration. She put the moonstone down, flexed her fingers, then picked it up again.

Terence hurried to her side. "You have to take it easy. This is the tricky part."

Again, Tink stopped. "I know," she said through gritted teeth.

Terence was too close. Tink was already nervous, and it didn't help to have him practically standing on her toes. Still, she told herself, he was only trying to help.

Once again, her fingers held the fragile moonstone as it hovered over the scepter.

Terence piped up. "Now we have to match the trajectory of the light beams with the—"

"Got it!" Tink snapped. She wished Terence would hush up and let her do her job.

But Terence was determined to continue advising. "With the—"

"I *know*!" Tink repeated.

Terence took a step even closer. "With the—"

"Shhh!" Tinker Bell said.

Terence refused to be shushed. "With the curvature of the moonstone."

Tink was so angry, her hands were shaking. "Will you *please* . . ."

As she spoke, one of the prongs for the setting fell off. Darn! It would have to be fixed or the moonstone wouldn't stay in place. Tinker Bell returned the stone to its case and closed it. She grabbed a stick and tried to fix the fallen prong by poking a hole in it. She jabbed and jabbed until the stick finally snapped.

Tinker Bell angrily threw down the stick. She closed her eyes and tried to take some deep breaths.

Terence picked up the scepter and studied the problem. "Looks like you need some sort of sharp thingy to fix this."

Tinker Bell's eyes flew open. "That's *exactly* what I need! Could you go out and find me something sharp?" she asked Terence.

"You got it," he said. "I'll be right back."

Terence flew out the door in a streak.

"Take your time," Tinker Bell called out after him, hoping he would be out looking for a long, long while.

Chapter Six

Meanwhile, at Tinkers' Nook, Clank was putting the finishing touches on his own new invention. He hammered a stake into the ground just as his friend Bobble came flying in with a set of bagpipes. "Clank, what is that?" Bobble asked.

"A fireworks launcher," Clank said proudly. "Iridessa and Rosetta will mix light crystals with flower pigment. The mixture will go into the launcher here. Then I tighten the spring, like so."

Clank loaded the launcher with the fireworks, not noticing that one of his feet was tangled in a coiled rope. "When you throw the trigger, the fireworks shoot into the air." He hit the launcher and the contraption sprang. The coiled rope tightened around Clank's leg and—*SPROING!*—hoisted him into the air, where he swung back and forth, dangling upside down from a tree branch. "Like soooooooooo," he concluded.

Bobble applauded. "Clanky, that's brilliant!"

Clank continued to swing, trying to decide whether or not to pretend he had done it on purpose, when Terence came flying over. "Hey, Bobble. Listen, do you know where I can find a sharp thingy?"

"A sharp thingy?" Bobble repeated.

"How about a stick?" Clank asked, swinging past Terence's head.

Terence looked around, unsure where the voice was coming from. "Huh? No, a sharp thingymajiggy."

Clank swung back the other way. "A stick can be pretty sharp."

"I need something to help Tink," Terence explained.

Clank swayed again. "Oh! For Tink? Did you try the cove?"

Terence snapped his fingers. "Of course! That's where all the Lost Things wash up. Thanks, Bobble. Thanks, Clank." Terence waved to them both and took off.

"Our pleasure," Bobble called out politely. "So long, Terence."

Clank decided that nothing really looked all that good upside down. "I'm getting a little dizzy," he announced. As the words were coming out of his mouth, the rope broke and he fell to the ground. "Ahhhhh! That's better," he said, grateful that matters had straightened themselves out so nicely.

"Perfect!" Tink stepped back and admired her work. With Terence out of the way, she was making speedy progress. Ever so carefully, she placed the moonstone on the scepter's tip. She blew on it and gave it a polish. "And now, for the finishing touch: a spattering of silver shavings."

Tinker Bell placed the scepter in a special stand made out of a spool and went to her supply chest to find some shavings.

She had just put her hand on a little box of spare shavings when she heard Terence. "Hey, Tink! I'm back!"

She turned and saw Terence rolling a huge compass through the door. "*What* is this?" she demanded.

"It's your sharp thingy," Terence said happily.

Tinker Bell could feel her temper rising, so she counted quickly. "Onetwothreefourfivesix . . ." It was no use; she was too mad. "Terence, this is not *sharp*. This is *round*. It is, in fact, the exact opposite of sharp."

Terence didn't seem to be listening. "But if you look inside, it's— "

Tinker Bell cut him off. "I need to work, okay? Now would you please get this thing out of here?" She bumped her hip against the compass to get it out of her way, and it began to roll . . . *straight toward the spool and the scepter!*

The compass knocked into the scepter, the scepter hit the floor, and the moonstone popped out and rolled across the room. Terence quickly leaned down and scooped it up. Across the room, the compass began to wobble like a coin standing on its edge.

Tinker Bell watched in horror as the compass fell sideways on top of the scepter, shattering it. The silver shavings fell from Tinker Bell's hands. "My scepter!"

"Tink," Terence pleaded. "I am so . . ."

Tink picked up a fragment of the broken scepter. So much work. So much time. So much care. And now . . . now it was all for nothing. And it was all Terence's fault. She snatched the moonstone from him and exploded. "*Out,* Terence! Just go!"

"What?"

"You! You brought this stupid thing here! You broke the scepter. This is your fault."

Terence stared at her in disbelief. "Tink, I was just trying to be a good friend."

"Go away! Leave me alone!"

Terence's face hardened. "Fine. And this is the last time I try to help you!" He flew out the door without so much as a backward glance.

Tink placed the moonstone safely on the soft cushion next to the fallen compass and began pacing. She was fuming. She looked at the calendar. Only a few more days left until the Autumn Revelry. *What* was she going to do?

Enraged, she hauled off and kicked the compass with all her strength. Mistake! Big mistake. "Ouch! Ouch! Ouch!" she cried. She hopped around in pain and then . . . *"Oh, no!"*

The compass cover popped open and landed right on the moonstone, breaking it to bits.

Tink's eyes grew large. Her heart pounded in her chest. "No!" she whispered, slumping to the floor. "No!"

This was a disaster beyond imagining. A catastrophe not just for Tinker Bell, but for all of Pixie Hollow. Without the scepter and the moonstone, there would be no blue pixie dust. The Pixie Dust Tree would perish. There would be no flying. No traveling to the mainland. No changes of seasons.

The world of fairies would come to an end.

What was she going to do?

Her eyes fell on her workbench and her scattered tools. She took a deep breath.

She would do the only thing she could do.

Get back to work.

Chapter Seven

Down at Lilypad Pond, Terence was trying to blow off steam by tossing some stones. "I kept her work space clean . . . brought her food . . . stoked the fire . . . searched high and low for a sharp thingy! And she didn't even say thank you."

The stone landed dangerously near a frog. The frog read Terence's mood and slipped away—out of range and out of danger.

Terence skimmed another rock, narrowly missing

Silvermist and a sparrow man, who were flying over the pond. "Whoa!" Silvermist protested.

Terence picked up the biggest rock he could find and tried to hurl it. But the rock was so large it sent him reeling backward.

Silvermist flew over and shook her head. "I know some rock fairies who are going to be pretty upset."

"There are no rock fairies," Terence grumbled.

"I know, but if there were, they'd be upset," Silvermist replied. "Are you okay?"

"Yeah, I'm great, why do you ask?" Terence said. He immediately regretted his sarcastic tone. "I'm sorry. I had a fight with Tink."

Silvermist sat down beside Terence. "What happened?"

"There was an accident. And she just exploded."

Silvermist turned pale. "She *exploded?*"

"No, no. I don't mean like that. I mean she yelled at me."

Silvermist chuckled. "Did she turn red?"

"Well, of course she turned red. It's Tink."

Silvermist waved her hand dismissively. "Just give her a chance to cool off."

Terence nodded. "Yeah. You're probably right,"

he agreed. But in his heart, he had his doubts. He glanced over his shoulder at Tink's house, wondering if the smoke he saw rising from the chimney was coming out of the fireplace—or out of Tink's ears.

Inside the house, Tinker Bell was hard at work. With great precision, she used a pair of tweezers to try to put the moonstone back together. She dipped a piece of broken moonstone in some sap and moved her magnifying glass for a better view. Carefully, very carefully, she tapped it and . . . the whole thing fell apart.

Tink hung her head in defeat. But she jerked it up when she heard a voice calling out to her.

"Hello, Tink!" Clank and Bobble were standing in the doorway.

Quick as lightning, Tink swept the moonstone fragments into a bag.

"We came to see if you wanted to join us for Fairy-Tale Theater," Clank said.

Bobble nodded. "We figure you could use a break."

"*Break?*" Tinker Bell squawked. "Nothing's broken. What do you mean? What do you know?" She saw their confused faces and caught herself. "Uh . . . sorry. Busy. You know, the revelry. Autumn Scepter and whatnot."

Clank grinned. "I can't wait to see that scepter! Is it as beautiful as I imagine?"

"Uhhhh . . ." Tink was at a loss for words.

Clank beamed. "Terence told us it's amazing. We are so proud of you."

Tinker Bell began gently herding them back through the door. "Look, guys, I really don't have time."

Bobble nodded. "Try not to worry, Tink. We'll tell Fairy Mary you couldn't make it."

"*Fairy Mary?*" Uh-oh! What did Bobble mean by that?

"Well, sure, you know her," Bobble said. "She never misses Fairy-Tale Theater. Bye-bye."

As soon as Clank and Bobble flew away, Tink

peered into the bag. She stared at the moonstone fragments and started thinking. Suddenly, she had an idea. "Clank! Bobble! Wait for me!" she shouted.

Tink soared out the door as fast as she could to catch up with her friends.

By the time she got to Fairy-Tale Glen, the place was packed. Tinker Bell made her way through the crowd until she found the head tinker. "Fairy Mary," she began in a breathless voice, "I—"

"Tinker Bell. I wasn't expecting to see you tonight. Have you finished the scepter?" Fairy Mary asked.

"Not exactly," Tinker Bell began. "I was wondering . . . I mean, I have to ask you—"

"Yes?"

"It's about the moonstone."

"What happened to it?"

"Errrr . . ."

"You didn't lose it? Tell me you didn't lose it."

"I didn't lose it."

"Oh, good."

"But I was thinking . . . if using one moonstone creates blue pixie dust, using two would create even more. Do you have another moonstone?"

Fairy Mary chuckled. "That moonstone is the only one found in the last one hundred years. And thank goodness we found it. Without the blue dust, the Pixie Dust Tree would grow weak. And things would be pretty tough around here, believe you me."

THUNK! Tink's legs turned to rubber and she fell backward.

Fairy Mary hurried to help her up. "Are you okay? You look sort of pale. Wait! I know what's going on!"

"You do?"

"You've been working too hard. What you need is a little theater. Knowing you, you'd probably redo the whole scepter if you could."

"Is that an option?" Tink asked with a nervous laugh.

The sound of chimes informed them that the

show was about to begin. It was time to find seats.

"Oh, Tink!" Fairy Mary laughed and grabbed Tinker Bell's hand, pulling her into the crowd.

Fairies poured into the woodland theater, eager to see Lyria, the most talented storyteller fairy. When everyone was seated, an animal fairy stood and struck up the bug and animal orchestra. Frogs, crickets, beetles, pill bugs, and centipedes played an introductory piece of music.

Music fairies played an overture with spider-silk harps, gourd timpani drums, and flower whistles. Light fairies arranged themselves overhead so that colorful beams streamed down and illuminated the orchestra and the stage.

Fairy Mary and Tinker Bell sat next to Bobble and Clank. Fairy Mary raised her opera glasses. "How exciting!"

Bobble put fresh droplets in his dewdrop goggles.

The chorus sang. *"Hush, fairies, shush, fairies, 'tis the moment for ancient fairy lore."*

The beautiful music made Tinker Bell feel even more depressed. She was about to slip away when her friend Fawn squeezed in between her and Fairy Mary. "Excuse me," Fawn whispered.

Tink's nose began to twitch. What was that smell? She glanced at Fawn and realized that she was looking a bit sheepish. The smell was coming from her. "Sorry," Fawn whispered. "Skunk training."

The music swelled. *"Aha, aha. Hush, fairies, shush, for a fairy tale of yore,"* sang the chorus.

The crowd held its breath in delighted anticipation . . . and gasped when an explosion of pixie dust materialized onstage. A rain of leaves came down, and Lyria appeared out of the whirling colors.

Lyria waved her hand, and a cloud of sparkling pixie dust formed animated images to illustrate her tale. A pirate ship appeared, flying over the audience. A crew of menacing pirates prowled along the aisles and converged onstage.

It was all part of the art of fairy stagecraft, but several of the bugs still dove behind a centipede for protection.

Lyria began her tale, holding the audience rapt. "'Twas a distant fall when a pirate ship arrived in Never Land. The dreaded pirates swarmed ashore, seeking the greatest and most elusive prize of all—a fairy."

Lyria focused her electric gaze on Bobble and—

POINK! POINK!—his eye-goggle droplets popped in fear.

Fawn clutched Tink's arm. "Pirates give me the willies," she whispered with a shudder.

Lyria waved her hand again, and the image of a fairy appeared. A giant hand came swooping down and snatched up the fairy. Lyria continued with the story. "Far and wide the pirates searched until they found a fairy. They chased her, captured her, and forced her to lead them to the most magical treasure of all—the enchanted Mirror of Incanta."

The image of an ornate hand mirror appeared in the air. "Forged by fairy magic in ages past, the mirror had the power to grant three wishes— anything precious to your heart."

Tink perked up, intrigued. "Fairy Mary," she whispered. "Is this true?"

"Every word," Fairy Mary confirmed.

Tink watched as the pixie dust ship Lyria had created crashed into jagged rocks. "The pirates used two wishes. But before they could use the third wish, the ship was wrecked on an island north of Never Land. The Mirror of Incanta, with its last remaining wish, was lost forever. Yet it is said that the clues to find it are hidden in this ancient chant."

Tink strained her ears, trying not to miss a word or a clue.

"Journey due north past Never Land, till a faraway island is close at hand."

Lyria created an image of an island. A cloud of butterfly wings transformed into a spooky set of eyes staring out of the darkness. On cue, an image of a stone arch appeared. *"When you're alone, but not alone, you will find help. And an arch of stone."*

Tink repeated the words so she would remember them. "Arch of stone," she whispered.

"There's one way across the isle's north ridge. But a price must be paid at the old troll bridge."

Lyria flew upward, and the image of two trolls running toward each other as if to fight appeared. When they collided, the image dissipated.

"What did she say?" Tink asked, trying to keep up with Lyria's clues.

"I think she said something about a toll bridge," Fawn answered.

"Toll bridge?"

Fawn nodded. "Yeah. But I don't know how much it costs."

Lyria walked the plank of the sparkling imaginary ship hovering in the air. *"At the journey's end, you shall walk the plank of the ship that sunk but never sank."*

Suddenly, the pirate ship was no longer in the air, but perched on a shore. Then it transformed into a satchel stamped with a skull and crossbones held up with a dagger. Then it turned into a pile of gems and jewels and the Mirror of Incanta. *"And in the hold, 'midst gems and gold, a wish-come-true awaits, we're told."*

Tink's mind was spinning. *Maybe there is a solution after all.* What luck that she had come to the play! That mirror, with its unused third wish, was the answer to her problem.

But she had to move fast. She feigned a yawn and slipped away. Vaguely, she heard the ominous warning at the end of Lyria's tale: *"But beware and be warned, there's a trick to this clue. Wish only goodwill, or no good will come you. For the treasure you seek may yet come to rue."*

Tinker Bell wasn't too worried. All treasure hunts and magic-wish schemes had traps associated with them. She didn't need to be warned about being careful. She would be the most careful treasure hunter and wish maker in history. She had to be. After all, she only had one chance. And she wasn't going to blow it.

Chapter Eight

Tink studied the huge compass that still sat in her home. The needle pointed north. What was it that Lyria had said? *"Faraway island is close at hand. Due north past Never Land."*

Tinker Bell found her map of Never Land and scanned it. There was an island north of Never Land, all right. And that was where she would go.

She checked her gear, making sure she had everything she would need—food, map, compass, sextant. She had put together a warmer outfit, with a hat and a cape. But then she realized she had another problem. "How am I going to carry all this?" she moaned. Pixie dust would lighten her load, but did she have enough to fly that far with this much stuff? She looked at her daily pixie dust supply. *Nope.*

Tink quickly left her house and flew to the Pixie Dust Distribution Depot. She looked around and saw Fairy Gary handing out the pixie dust rations to some fairies. "There you go. One cup, dear." The fairies thanked Fairy Gary and flew away. Tink immediately took her place at the end of the line and smiled. "Hi, Fairy Gary."

"Hello, Tink. What brings you here?" Fairy Gary asked.

Tink hated to come right out and ask for more dust. The rules were very strict. She decided to butter him up first. "I see that bucket-and-pulley system I rigged up for you is working out. You know, you really run a tight ship." She smiled at him, trying to get on his good side. "I know it sounds like I'm just saying it. But you really do. Really."

Fairy Gary blushed with pride. "That's very

sweet, dear. Ho, ho, ho, ho!" he chuckled.

"Anyway," Tink went on, "I was wondering . . . canIhavesomeextrapixiedust?" She hoped that if she said it really fast he might say yes before he realized what she was asking.

"Ho, ho, ho—pardon?" Fairy Gary did a double take.

"Come on, Fairy Gary. Please. Just a smidge."

"Now, Tinker Bell, you know the rules." He consulted his checklist. "It says here you have already had your daily ration."

Tinker Bell flew away without even saying good-bye. She saw Iridessa, Rosetta, and Silvermist passing overhead and took off after them. Maybe they could help her.

"Iridessa! Rosetta! Silvermist!" Very quickly, Tink explained that she needed some dust for a special project that she couldn't discuss. But her friends were as shocked by her request as Fairy Gary had been.

"Lend you some of our dust!" Iridessa exclaimed. "Tinker Bell! We need every bit of it on the mainland."

Rosetta nodded. "It takes a lot of flying to bring

in autumn, sweetie. Sorry," she added regretfully.

Rosetta and Iridessa flew off to take care of business, but Silvermist lingered. "Say, you know who might be able to help?"

Tinker Bell knew she was talking about Terence. She and Terence weren't exactly on the best of terms right now. Still, maybe he would help her. She blew out a sigh that sent her bangs flying straight up. It was worth a try.

"Rafaela . . . Renato . . . Redina . . . Rina . . ." Terence had grumpily checked his list and was flying out of the depot, ready to make his pixie dust deliveries, when he heard a happy squeak. It was Cheese the mouse pulling Fawn in a cart. They drove by and gave him a cheerful wave.

Terence didn't feel very cheerful, but he tried to fake it—flashing them a smile and a wave. "Hi,

Cheese. Good morning, Fawn." As soon as they were around the corner, he let his face fall back into its gloomy expression. He returned to his list but was startled when he heard somebody at his elbow.

"Terence!"

He turned. "Tinker Bell!" Why had she come? To yell at him some more? Well, she could scream all she wanted. He didn't care what she did anymore. "I'm surprised to see you here. How's the scepter?" he asked coldly.

"I'm working on it," she replied. Her eyes darted around and she seemed nervous. Clearly, there was something on her mind. "Look, Terence. Things happened. Mistakes were made. Um, there's something I need to talk to you about."

Terence felt his anger melt away. Tinker Bell could get mad and blow up, but she always apologized. And when she did, he was ready to forgive—one hundred percent. No hard feelings. Terence waited.

"I need some extra pixie dust," she blurted out, thrusting a bag toward him.

Terence couldn't believe it. Surely she was kidding. He looked at the bag and then at Tink.

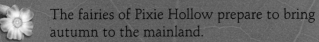

The fairies of Pixie Hollow prepare to bring autumn to the mainland.

Iridessa changes the color of the leaves.

Fawn helps a bird come in for a safe landing.

Silvermist and Fairy Mary prepare for the
Autumn Revelry.

Tinker Bell tests her new invention—a boat named the *Pixie Dust Express*.

Fairy Mary, the Minister of Autumn, and Queen Clarion show Tink the Hall of Scepters—and ask her to make the new Autumn Scepter.

 Tink shows Terence the rare and precious moonstone.

Tink's Autumn Scepter gets crushed by a heavy compass. Her hard work is ruined!

 As if things weren't bad enough, the moonstone shatters, too!

Tink flies off in search of the Mirror of Incanta.

Tinker Bell meets a firefly named Blaze.

Tink and Blaze are helped along their journey by some friendly insects.

Tink and Blaze find the troll bridge—and the angry trolls who guard it!

Tink and Blaze discover the pirate shipwreck. The Mirror of Incanta waits somewhere inside.

Terence arrives just in time to help Tink
escape from the pirate ship!

Tink prepares to show her Autumn Scepter
to all the fairies of Pixie Hollow!

Nope. She was serious. "You need more pixie dust? That's why you're here?" he asked, stunned.

Tinker Bell nodded.

"That's not exactly what I was expecting. Why do you need more dust?"

"I can't tell you."

"You can't tell me? You need more pixie dust and you can't tell me why?" Terence was trying very hard to wrap his mind around this. As he watched, he could see Tink turning red, which meant her temper was rising. Boy, did she have some nerve or what!

"A true friend wouldn't ask!" she shouted.

That did it. "A true friend wouldn't ask me to break the rules!" he shouted back.

"Then I guess we're not true friends!" she yelled, turning her back to him.

Terence couldn't believe it. "I guess we're not," he whispered.

"I'm on my own, then," Tinker Bell said, flying away.

Terence watched her go, feeling his heart harden again—this time for good. *Some friend,* he thought. *With friends like that, who needs enemies?*

As Tinker Bell flew away, figuring out a way to fix the moonstone was all she could think about. Her heart felt as hard as steel.

Desperate times called for desperate measures. An idea began forming in her brain. A plan. An invention. A contraption. A way out of this horrible mess *that was all Terence's fault*. She sprang into feverish action, flying here and there, gathering everything she would need all over Pixie Hollow.

By late afternoon, Tink had found cotton from the cotton-ball fields, feathers from reluctant bird donors, the gourd she had made her boat from, and all manner of tools, screws, odds, ends, bits, pieces, and whatnots.

Then she went to work. Hammering, nailing, sawing, screwing, gluing, measuring, hanging, and hoping.

By evening, her contraption was complete. Dressed in her adventuring outfit, Tinker Bell stood back and took a moment to admire the balloon and the basket that would carry her north in search of the enchanted mirror.

She had crafted the balloon out of cotton balls. The hollowed-out gourd formed the basket. Pots and pans hung from the sides to provide ballast. She would drop them as she traveled to make the balloon lighter as the pixie dust began to lose strength.

She didn't have much pixie dust, but what she had—combined with the cotton balls, wind, and clever management of her ballast—would have to be enough to lift her into the sky and carry her where she needed to go.

Tink sprinkled the cotton with a bit of pixie dust, grabbed her provisions, and pulled up the anchor.

Up went the balloon.

Up high over Pixie Hollow.

Up over the hilltops.

Up, up, up Tinker Bell went.

And then . . . *away!*

Chapter Nine

As day turned to night and the sky darkened, Tink relied on her sextant to get her bearings. "I just need to angle the moon with the horizon," she muttered, mainly to reassure herself that she was perfectly capable of making this trip on her own. *What difference does it make if it is pitch-black dark?* she thought. *What difference does it make if I am by myself? What diff—Oh, no! What is that?*

A glowing mass in the distance was heading

straight for her. It was a swarm of fireflies. A swarm of fireflies being pursued by a *bat*!

ZOOM! ZIP! WHIZ!

The swarm swept past Tink like a tiny hurricane of shooting stars. She ducked this way and that. *BUMP!* A baby firefly smacked right into the rope. Tink moved to help him.

"Yeow!" She quickly ducked when the bat came swooping over the top of the gourd basket, narrowly missing her.

Tink slowly lifted her head. The bat was gone. So was the baby firefly. Tink swallowed hard, hoping the firefly had avoided becoming the bat's dinner. She checked the ropes on her balloon and adjusted her course, dropping a few pots and pans to get a little more lift.

Once her nerves began to calm, she realized that the flutter in her stomach wasn't just fear. "I'm starving!" she said in surprise. She leaned over and opened one of her supply bags. It was empty. "My boysenberry rolls! What happened to them?" She reached into another supply bag and heard a growl from inside.

Alarmed, Tink withdrew her hand. *What in the*

world? She leaned down to see what was in her bag. Suddenly, a light shone in her face, blinding her. "Ahh!" Tink stumbled back as the bag jiggled.

She grabbed a large stick. Very carefully, she poked the bag and lifted the top. She peered inside and her mouth fell open.

Inside the bag was the baby firefly. His stomach bulged and he let out a contented burp. Tink picked up the bag and dumped him out, along with a batch of crumbs. "My cheese! My pumpernickel muffin!"

She glared at the fat little firefly. She'd been worried that he had been eaten by the bat. Judging by this guy's appetite, though, it was probably the bat who should have been worried!

Tink picked the firefly up and set him outside her now-empty food bag. "Out! Shoo! Go find your friends." She gave him a little push, but the firefly fluttered at the edge of the basket.

"Stop following me. I'm on a very important mission. I have two days to find the magic mirror and wish the moonstone back."

The firefly saluted, as if to offer his services.

"No," Tinker Bell said. "I don't need any help." She turned her back and studied the map.

The firefly refused to be ignored. He hovered beside her, inching closer and closer until his glowing behind was right between her face and the map. Tink sighed. Now what?

Her eye rested on a stick. Aha! She grabbed the stick and shook it teasingly. "Hey, look. Look, little guy. Now, fetch!" Tink tossed the stick out into the night. The firefly took off after it, his bright light disappearing into the dark sky.

Tink smiled and turned back to her map. "Ahh!" she yelled again. The firefly was already back with the stick. She tried to tug it away from him, but he held on. "Will you please get out of here?" she begged.

Without warning, the firefly let go of the stick. Tink tumbled backward, windmilling her arms to keep her balance. The stick caught the pouch of precious pixie dust and sent it flying overboard.

"No!" Tink yelled. She jumped out of the basket and dove after it. Down, down, down she went, spinning and buzzing. Finally, she was able to grab the bag, slow her descent, and fly back. Once inside the basket, she glared at the firefly. It was like having another Terence around. She put her hands on her

hips. "Out!" She pointed away from the balloon.

The firefly's wings drooped. His face fell. Sadly, he walked along the edge of the gourd basket as if he were walking a plank. He looked back over his shoulder at Tink.

Tink crossed her arms. She was determined not to cave in.

The firefly resumed his walk, wiggled his glowing backside, and then jumped.

Tink hurried to the edge and looked out in every direction to make sure he was gone. He was. Good. Now maybe she could figure out where she was. She picked up the map and squinted at it. Boy, without the little firefly around, things sure were a whole lot darker.

Suddenly, the map began to glow. Was it magic? No! It was the firefly. Tink lowered the map and found herself looking into the bug's pleading eyes.

"Ohhhhh, all right," she said. "You can stay. For now."

He bounced around her like a happy puppy—capering, careening, and licking her face. Once he calmed down, Tinker Bell adjusted his position as if he were a lamp. "Just do me a favor. Stay riiiight here. If my bearings are accurate, we should see land soon."

If they were going to be traveling companions, Tinker Bell decided, they needed to introduce themselves. "I'm Tinker Bell. What's your name?"

The firefly blazed his light brighter. "Blinky? Flicker?" she guessed.

The firefly didn't look pleased.

"Flash? Beam?" Still no enthusiasm. "Flare?"

Now the little firefly looked downright cross.

"Well, how in the blazing bellows am I supposed to guess your name if—" Suddenly, the firefly perked up and quickly circled around Tink's head. She realized she was close.

"That's it! You're Blaze. Hmmm. Kind of a tough-guy name. Are you a tough guy?"

Blaze struck a pose with his dukes up. But he didn't look the least bit fierce. He looked as cute as . . . well . . . a baby firefly. Tinker Bell chuckled. "Okay, don't hurt yourself, tough guy."

Blaze dropped his fists and smiled happily, his little taillight glowing with happiness.

Chapter Ten

The next day, back in Pixie Hollow, the woods were abuzz with preparations for the revelry. Fairy Mary flew from one workplace to the next, her checklist in hand. So much to do. So little time.

She watched with approval as Cheese the mouse trotted along, pulling a cart filled with lanterns. Iridessa fluttered above. They worked efficiently as a team, hanging the lanterns among the trees.

"That's it, keep them coming," Iridessa urged.

Cheese snatched a lantern with his tail and flung it into the air. Iridessa skillfully caught it and hung it from a branch. "Got it. Next."

"Iridessa, how are those lanterns holding out?" Fairy Mary called.

Her voice distracted Iridessa, and she missed the next lantern as it came flying up. Luckily, the lantern looped around and hooked itself onto the branch at the exact right spot.

"Good shot, Cheese," Iridessa said. She turned to Fairy Mary. "We're almost done with the lanterns. Then I'll get Rosetta some light crystals for the fireworks."

Fairy Mary nodded and went to check on Rosetta. The garden fairy sat on the ground, grinding flower petals into pigment with a mortar and pestle. "I can't wait to mix them with my begonias, gardenias, and . . . ummmm . . ." Rosetta wrinkled her forehead and snapped her fingers, trying to remember what the next flower was. Luckily, a sparrow man came flying behind her and was able to supply the answer. "Forget-me-nots," he said.

"Forget-me-nots. Right. I keep forgetting those."

Clearly, Rosetta had things under control in her

department. Fairy Mary turned her attention to Fawn, who was coaching a flock of butterflies on a bush. "Fawn, show me how that twenty-one-butterfly salute is coming along."

Fawn turned toward the butterflies. "All right, fellas, when I blow the whistle, you guys go. On your mark, get set—"

But before Fawn could blow the whistle, the butterflies fluttered away in random directions—all except for one obedient little butterfly who sat at attention, patiently waiting for the signal.

Fawn blew the whistle and off he went. She sighed. "One down and twenty to go," she told Fairy Mary.

Fairy Mary chuckled. "Keep at it," she said in an encouraging voice. Fairy Mary knew that teaching butterflies wasn't easy. They tended to be . . . well . . . flighty. "Silvermist," she asked, "what are you working on?"

"Pollywog bubbles." Silvermist beckoned Fairy Mary over to observe. The water fairy held a twig bubble-blower over a water barrel. "Okay, guys," she said. The tadpoles in the barrel began to blow bubbles in unison. All except the smallest one.

The little tadpole took a big breath and blew. A large bubble surrounded him and he began to float upward. The tadpole stared out from the bubble in surprise and bewilderment. Silvermist reached up and poked the bubble. *POP!* Then . . . *PLOP!* The tadpole fell into her arms. She gently put him back in the barrel. "There you go," she said with a laugh.

"Nicely done," Fairy Mary told her. Then she went to check on the fireworks launcher. She could see Clank and Bobble on the other side of the field, working hard. *Good sparrow men, both,* she thought. *But they often need very close watching.* "Is it ready yet?" Fairy Mary called out.

Clank nodded enthusiastically.

"Let 'er rip," Bobble commanded.

Clank took a big swing at the rope trigger and . . . *BOING!*

"Arghghghghg!" The catapult scooped Bobble up and flung him through the air, where he—*SMACK!*—collided with a flower, making it fall backward. "I'm okay," he called out to Fairy Mary.

But as she watched, the flower sprang forward, sending Bobble flying back. Fairy Mary covered her eyes. She couldn't watch. But she could hear the

CRASH! BANG! BOOM! of Bobble falling right into the jumble of building supplies. "Still okay," she heard Bobble call out again, though his voice was considerably weaker.

Fairy Mary let out a sigh. *Oh, well,* she reflected. *Dress rehearsals never go well.* Everything would fall into place when the time came. And no matter what happened with the butterflies, tadpoles, or fireworks, at least the scepter would be a success.

Tinker Bell was volatile, but she was also talented and dedicated. The new scepter was sure to be the most beautiful and magical ever designed. And the tinker fairies would have good reason to be proud.

By sunset, Tink was journeying across the sea in her balloon. Time was running out. Only two more days until the Autumn Revelry. "I don't understand, Blaze. We should have seen land by now."

Blaze was sympathetic but sleepy. He yawned. "You go ahead and get some rest," Tinker Bell said. "I'll take the first watch."

Blaze didn't need to be told twice. He immediately curled up on a bag and fell asleep. His light flickered on and off in time with his gentle snoring.

Tink took the rudder and stared out into the dark sky, trying to discern some sign of land. All she saw was the moonlight reflecting on the ocean surface below.

Soon the soft rhythm of Blaze's snores began to lull her, and as the balloon headed into a large fogbank, her head tipped down and she fell fast asleep.

BANG!

"I'm awake! I'm awake!" Tinker Bell yelled in startled surprise. She rubbed the sleep from her eyes. It was daytime, and the balloon had just collided with something. But what?

She looked over the side of the basket. "I'm in a tree. This must be the lost island!" she cried. She rubbed her eyes again and stared hard into the distance, where she was pretty sure she saw an arch. "There it is! The stone arch from the story!"

Thrilled, Tink grabbed the anchor and hurled it off the balloon, watching as it hooked itself onto a branch. She turned to Blaze. "You stay here and guard the balloon. I'll be right back."

Without waiting for an answer, Tink took off, flying as fast as she could toward the arch.

She got closer . . . and closer . . . and closer. Suddenly, she had a clear view of the "arch." "No!" she wailed. Without the mist and the blur of sleep in her eyes, she could see that the arch was not an archway made of stone—it was only two dead trees twisted together. Her eyes had been playing tricks on her.

She heard Blaze buzzing behind her. "Not now," she said, trying to brush him away. "This is supposed to be a rock arch. Not a twisty, branchy tree arch."

Blaze circled Tink's head in a tizzy, but she ignored him. She needed to think. Now what? She had come all this way and had no idea which direction to take.

Blaze became more persistent, pulling and pulling at her hair. "What has gotten into you?" she demanded, whirling around to glance at him. Then she saw what he was trying to tell her. "Blaze!" she gasped. "Where's the balloon?"

Blaze launched into an elaborate pantomime, pointing into the distance and pretending to blow with the wind.

"It's gone? My compass? My supplies? My pixie dust? Why didn't you warn me?"

Blaze rolled his eyes and cocked his head, as if to say, "What do you think I've been trying to do?"

Tinker Bell felt her face get flushed. She hated it when other fairies—or bugs—were right. "Okay. Okay. We'll get back to that later. Right now we've got to catch that balloon." Tink fanned her wings and took off, with Blaze flying close beside her.

The wind was definitely blowing hard, and Tink could see why the balloon had sailed away. A leaf came tumbling through the air and smacked the little firefly.

"Blaze!" Tinker Bell cried. She turned to check on her friend and a second leaf smacked right into her, knocking her backward. Tink peeled it away, still going as fast as she could, only to fly into a thick branch. *WHAM!* She hit her head, hard, and the next thing she knew, the whole world went black.

Chapter Eleven

When Tink came to, she was groggy, and in a forest. She sat up and looked around. To her amazement, she saw Terence and the compass. They were only a few feet away. Terence started toward her. "Tink. I'm so sorry. I—"

"Terence," Tink gasped. "How did you get here?"

Terence didn't answer—because he wasn't really there.

Tinker Bell was lying on the floor of the forest

with a big bump on her head. As if by some strange magic, she felt as if she had traveled back in time. She was watching Terence and herself arguing in her house.

She saw the broken pieces of the scepter on the floor. "You! You brought this stupid thing here!" she shouted at Terence. "You broke the scepter. This is your fault."

Terence looked stricken and sad. "Tink, I was just trying to be a good friend."

"Go away!" Tinker Bell yelled. "Leave me alone!"

Terence's face turned from sad to angry. "Fine. And this is the last time I try to help you!" He opened his wings and flew away, disappearing into the clouds.

Tinker Bell immediately regretted her angry words. "Terence. Terence. No. Come back. Don't leave. Don't leave. Don't . . ."

Suddenly, she realized that she wasn't really watching Terence or herself. She hadn't really traveled back in time. She had been dreaming. Now she was awake, alone, and calling out for Terence.

She shook her head to clear it. What had happened? The she remembered—she had been chasing her balloon and had hit a tree. "Blaze! Where are you? Blaze?"

Tinker Bell's heart began to sink. She had been pretty harsh with Blaze. Maybe he had run away from her, too, just like Terence.

But Blaze buzzed over and hovered at her side. Tink threw her arms around him, glad of the little bug's company. "Oh, Blaze, what am I going to do? I lost my balloon. I lost my pixie dust. I'm starving. What have I done?"

Blaze wriggled out of her grasp and zoomed away.

Tinker Bell dropped her face into her hands. Blaze was abandoning her, too. She really didn't blame him. She'd botched things up. Why would he feel any loyalty to her? Suddenly, something brushed up against Tinker Bell's ankle and she let out a shriek.

She looked down and saw that it was only a harmless pill bug! Startled by her cry, he curled up into a tight ball.

Tinker Bell's face turned red. How embarrassing! But it was only natural to be nervous. After all, she was alone in a strange forest.

But when Tink lifted her eyes, her brows flew upward in amazement. *She wasn't alone.* In fact, she was surrounded by friendly butterflies, ladybugs, bees, and more pill bugs. Blaze hadn't abandoned her—he had gone out and gathered up as much company to comfort her as he could find.

Tink gave the little pill bug that had startled her a pat. He uncurled himself and crawled into her lap. A group of bees came flying over and offered her a large honeycomb. "Oh!" Tinker Bell smiled. "Thank you." She quickly swallowed several big drops of the sweet honey.

Another pill bug inched forward, balancing a leaf filled with fresh dew. Tink scooped it up and drank it down. *Ahhh!* Her thirst was immediately quenched.

Refreshed, Tinker Bell began to feel better. She beamed at her bug companions. "Wow. That hit the spot. Thank you so much."

Blaze buzzed around, blinking his light to signal his happiness.

Tinker Bell leaned down and drew a picture of the arch in the dirt. "We're lost," she told her new friends, hoping they'd be able to help. "By any chance, have you seen a stone arch around here?"

A huge swarm of bees lifted Tinker Bell to her feet and pushed her in the direction of the jungle. All the bugs and butterflies hovered and buzzed, urging her to fly. But Tinker Bell couldn't get off the ground. "Oh, no! I'm out of pixie dust. Looks like I'll be walking from here."

She spotted something on the ground. "My compass!" She ran to it. It had obviously fallen out of the balloon basket when it had drifted away. Now it lay in pieces on the ground. She leaned over to inspect it. *"Ouch!"* She accidentally poked herself with the needle. *Now* she understood why Terence had brought her the compass. "That *is* a sharp thingy, Terence," she muttered. She stuck the needle in her belt. A sharp thingy was always handy to have on an adventure.

The bugs began moving, and Tink followed. They led her through the forest to an outcropping of rock that overlooked a valley. Ta-da! Tink looked across the valley, and there it was. "The stone arch! Blaze, we made it. We're here."

One of the pill bugs rubbed up against her ankle. Grateful for his help, Tink leaned over and gave him a pat on the head. "Thank you so much."

Tinker Bell and Blaze waved good-bye to the bugs and set out in the direction of the arch. "Great to have friends who'll help you out, huh?" she whispered to him.

Even though she had every reason to be happy, she couldn't help feeling sad. She had once had a friend back home who would help her, too. Tinker Bell bowed her head in sorrow. That friendship was over now.

Back in Pixie Hollow, Terence sat with his own head bowed. He needed some advice. "I know Tink is my best friend," he said sadly. "We should just forgive each other. Someone just needs to take the first step."

"Who?" Terence's companion asked.

"I think it should be Tink," Terence said promptly.

"Who?"

"Tink. She blamed me for breaking the scepter."

"Who?"

Terence looked up and met his companion's gaze. His companion blinked and turned his head all the way around. *Owls really are amazing,* Terence thought.

"Who?" the owl asked again. He looked straight at Terence. "Who?"

Terence began to understand. *He* should be the one to go to Tinker Bell. "Me," Terence answered. "Me!" A smile spread across his face. "Thank you so much, Mr. Owl. You know what? You truly *are* the wisest of all the creatures."

Terence flew toward Tink's house. He needed to talk to her.

He took a deep breath and knocked on the door. "Hey, Tink! It's me. Look, I know you're mad at me. But there's something I need to tell you."

Terence waited, but there was no answer from inside the house.

Cautiously, he opened the door. "Anyone home?"

Still no answer. Terence entered the house and shut the door behind him. There was a strange, musty stillness in the air. He stepped carefully over the broken pieces of the scepter that had caused so much trouble between him and Tink.

Something glittering on the floor drew his attention. His eyes widened. He kneeled down and scooped up a handful of dust. He examined it closely and gasped. *Oh, no!* In the dust he could clearly see tiny pieces of the moonstone.

That could only mean one thing: The moonstone had broken.

This was a disaster. A tragedy. He looked around. No wonder the house was empty. Tink was gone. But where?

Terence went to her desk, looking for clues. As soon as he saw her diagram for a balloon and a checklist of things to take, he understood the situation. It wasn't good.

Tink had sailed away in a homemade balloon— and she was alone.

Tinker Bell trudged through the valley. Her heart felt almost as heavy as her feet. "It's our last day, Blaze. We've got to find that shipwreck soon."

They came to the edge of a chasm. Though Tinker Bell was out of pixie dust, there were always a few specks clinging to a fairy's wings. Tink fanned her wings as hard as she could and felt a little lift.

She flung herself forward and held her breath. She barely managed to get across the chasm. Her hands scrambled wildly to hold on and keep her from slipping off the edge. As soon as she was on her feet again, Blaze let out a squeak and pointed to a tunnel.

A tunnel? Tink didn't remember anything about a tunnel in Lyria's story. But all tunnels led somewhere, and Tink had nothing left to lose. So she took a deep breath and dove into the dark opening with Blaze right behind her.

Chapter Twelve

When Tink and Blaze came out the other end of the tunnel, they found themselves in a thick forest. A covered bridge encrusted with thorny thickets stretched out ahead of them. Two stone trolls guarded the entrance.

Tink put one foot on the bridge and the trolls sprang to life. She drew back, alarmed.

"None shall pass the secret troll bridge," the tall one intoned.

Tinker Bell smacked her head. "*Troll* bridge. I thought Lyria said *toll* bridge." She tried to laugh, and Blaze displayed his most engaging smile. "Look, fellas. I don't want any trouble."

The tall troll glared. "We are guardians—"

The short troll cut him off. "Hey, hey, hey."

The tall troll plowed on. ". . . of the secret—"

"Hey!" the small troll barked again.

"What?" the tall troll asked irritably.

"It's my turn to give the ominous warning, blockhead."

"Is not," responded the tall troll.

"Is too," said the short one.

"Is not," repeated the tall troll.

"Is too."

"Not."

"Too."

"Not! Not! Not!"

"Too! Too! Too!"

"But you did it last time," protested the tall troll.

The short troll looked indignant. "That was over three hundred years ago."

The tall troll grudgingly relented. "Go ahead," he said gruffly.

The short troll squared his shoulders and cleared his throat. "We are guardians of the secret bridge. Beat it before we grind your bones to make our bed."

"Bread," the tall troll corrected.

"What?"

The tall troll rolled his eyes. "The expression is 'grind your bones to make our *bread*.' Not *bed*."

"Really? Who would want to make bread out of bones? Might break a tooth."

The tall troll began to lose his patience. "Well, who'd want to sleep in a bed made of bones? Hard on the back. That'd put a crick in your neck, you knucklehead."

The small troll seemed to remember that Tinker Bell and Blaze were watching and listening. "Ixnay in front of the ictim-vay, gravel-for-brains."

The tall troll was too insulted to worry about what Tinker Bell and Blaze thought about them. He was just eager to hurl an insult back. "Fuzz Face."

"Thimblehead."

"Stinky Breath."

"Googly Eyes."

"Waxy Ears!"

"Unibrow!" the small troll bellowed.

Tinker Bell and Blaze looked at each other in disbelief. These two were clearly not serious about guarding the bridge. If they wanted to waste time standing here and trading insults, that was their business. But Tink had a magic mirror to find. She started forward. "Excuse me. I need to get through!"

The two trolls snapped to attention. "None shall pass!" they proclaimed in what sounded like an official troll voice.

Now Tink was mad. If these two goofballs thought they were going to stop her, they had another think coming. Tink put her hands on her hips and thrust her face forward. "Do you have any idea what I've been through here? I almost got attacked by bugs and bats, and got blown all over the place by the wind, and almost starved to death to find a mirror that grants one last wish—which I wouldn't have even needed if Terence had taken his time finding me a sharp thingy instead of making me break the moonstone. And then he didn't even share his pixie dust because he cares more about the stupid rules than he does about me. And if that wasn't enough, he even went and tried—"

"Whoa! Whoa!" cautioned the tall troll,

interrupting. "Hang on. Hang on. Who's Terence?"

"Is he a friend of yours?" asked the small troll.

"Well, yeah. He was my best friend."

"But you're not very nice," commented the tall troll.

"Hey. Don't you judge me. You've been yelling at each other since I got here." She looked over at Blaze to make sure he was still with her.

Blaze crossed his six arms over his body and nodded at Tink—letting her know that he had her back.

"He knows I don't mean it." The tall troll looked at the short one. "Don't you?"

The small troll gave him a sentimental smile. "You old softie."

The tall troll smiled, too. "Like when I call you Wart Face."

"Or when I called you Big Nose."

"Booger Breath." This time, there was a little edge in the tall troll's voice.

"Stinky Feet."

Now the tall troll was genuinely annoyed. "Weasel Toes!" he said, daring the small troll to try to top that.

The small troll hit right back with "Badger Brain!"

"Garden Gnome," the tall troll thundered, delivering what was clearly the most annihilating insult in the troll arsenal.

The small troll seemed to crumble. His face fell. His eyes filled with tears. "Garden Gnome," he whispered, as if he just couldn't believe that his oldest and dearest friend could have said something so hurtful.

The tall troll was immediately apologetic: "Oh, dear. I don't know where that came from. I . . . I . . . crossed the line."

"Say the magic words," sniffled the small troll. "Go on."

The tall troll looked around as if to be sure no one could overhear.

Tinker Bell eagerly leaned forward, determined to catch what they were saying. *Magic words!* Maybe they were the magic words she would need to speak to the Mirror of Incanta.

The tall troll finally spoke. "I'm sorry," he said, giving the words great weight and emphasis.

"Do you mean it?" the small troll asked weakly.

"Absolutely."

"Do you feel it?" pressed the small troll.

"Deeply."

The small troll considered it; then he smiled broadly. "Then I forgive you."

"Friends?" the tall troll asked.

"Friends," the small troll confirmed. "Come here, buddy."

"Pal."

Even though those weren't the magic words Tinker Bell had been hoping for, she couldn't help smiling as she watched the curmudgeonly trolls embrace. It was a terrible thing to see good friends fight.

"Amigo!" the small troll said happily.

"Compadre!" cried the tall one.

"You're the best."

"No, you."

"No, *you!*"

Blaze nudged Tink and flickered his light. She gave him a nod. Now was the time to cross the bridge—while the two trolls were paying more attention to each other than to her.

"You're right," the tall troll said, switching tactics.

"I *am* the best," he said with a sly smile.

The small troll rose immediately to the bait. "So now you think you're better than me?"

Quietly, Tinker Bell began to tiptoe past them, leaving the trolls to enjoy their favorite activity—bickering.

Chapter Thirteen

Tinker Bell and Blaze pushed forward on their journey. It was a long and exhausting haul. With every passing hour, Tink became more and more anxious. Time was slipping away. If they didn't find the mirror soon, it would be too late.

"Blaze!" she said suddenly. "Listen!"

She heard the unmistakable sound of surf breaking on a beach. She lurched forward, plowing through brush and branches until she finally came upon a breathtaking sight: a jagged, rock-strewn beach . . . *with the remains of a wrecked ship washed up on the shore.*

"'The ship that sunk but never sank.' Blaze, this is it!" She ran toward the hulk with Blaze flying behind her. "We've got to find that mirror and fix the moonstone."

The closer she got to the wreck, the spookier it looked. She approached with caution. The ship looked as if it were haunted. Barnacles clung to the beams. Cobwebs draped over every surface. Rotten ropes and rusted pulleys swayed in the breeze, groaning and squeaking.

She stepped inside and shivered from the cold. "Why couldn't the mirror be in a bunny-filled meadow?" she muttered, then stopped with a gasp. There was a monster's shadow on the wall in front of her!

Blaze saw the shadow, too, and immediately lifted his fists, ready to fight.

But then Tink smiled. She realized that the monstrous shadow was actually the result of Blaze's light shining on the walls of the ship. Tinker Bell made growling sounds and moved Blaze back and forth so that his light created a shadow-puppet show.

They both laughed, but abruptly stopped as their playful giggling echoed through the ship, turning into a maniacal cackle.

Now they were too frightened to laugh. But the trick of the light gave Tink an idea. She took off her headband and wrapped it around Blaze so that she could direct the beam he was making. Blaze, always happy to help, shone as brightly as he could.

They climbed through the ship, making their way to the captain's quarters. The farther into the ship they went, the darker and scarier it got. Tink tried to ignore the thundering beat of her own heart. They edged along broken ledges and rotten floorboards. Finally, they entered the captain's bedroom. The once-grand chamber was littered with cobwebs, barnacles, tattered wall hangings, and rusted iron furniture.

Tink moved Blaze around and peered into the corners. "Look, Blaze!" she cried. High up, hanging from a dagger plunged into the wall, was a satchel stamped with a skull and crossbones.

Tinker Bell fanned her wings and tried desperately to reach it, but she couldn't. She drew the compass needle from her belt and thrust it at the satchel like a spear.

The spear struck the satchel and ripped a hole in its side. A river of precious objects poured out of the hole. Tink had to jump aside quickly to avoid being crushed by the falling stream of treasure—most of it clearly stolen from fairies. Tiny silver looms, gold caps, rings, cups, vases, shoes, and paintings fell in a mound. A fairy-sized ring bounced off Tink's head. She caught it and slipped it on her finger. Nice. But she wasn't here to find jewelry.

She stared at the huge twinkling pile. "What do you think, Blaze? Could the mirror be in there? Help me look." The firefly hovered overhead as Tink pawed through the loot. She drew back and gasped when she found something absolutely astonishing.

She saw her own face staring back at her with enormous eyes and a mouth wide open. The face looked as surprised as Tink felt.

This could only mean one thing.

Tink was looking at a mirror!

"It's for real!" she exclaimed. She picked up the looking glass. The gold handle and seashell frame were embellished with precious pink pearls.

Tinker Bell tried to stay calm. The solution to her problem was finally in her hands. All she had to do now was repair the moonstone. She removed the fragments from her own satchel and laid them carefully in front of the mirror.

"Okay, deep breath," she told herself. "Clear your mind. You only get one shot at this. Here goes."

Tink lifted the mirror. She looked directly at her reflection and was just about to speak when . . .

BZZZZZZ! Blaze flew right past her ear.

Tink shook her head to clear it and prepared to start over. "I wish . . ."

BZZZZZZ! BZZZZZZ! BZZZZZZ! Blaze flew around Tinker Bell's head in giddy excitement. *Good grief!* Blaze was as distracting as Terence. *Can't he see that I'm trying to concentrate?*

"I wish—" she began again.

BZZZZZZ! BZZZZZZ! BZZZZZZ!

Tinker Bell whipped her head around. "I wish you'd be quiet for one minute!" she blurted out.

Instantly, the buzzing stopped and Tink's irritation subsided. "Thank you." She turned back to the mirror and watched her own expression turn to one of shock when she realized what she had just done.

Horrified, she looked back at Blaze, who continued to fly in circles . . . *making absolutely no sound at all.*

Tink's eyes widened with dread. "No! No! No! No!" Her hands gripped the mirror and throttled the handle until her knuckles turned white. "I take that wish back. Please! Don't let it count. That wasn't my wish."

She whirled around and lashed out at Blaze. "Look what you've done! This mirror was my last chance. This is all your fault!"

Her shoulders slumped. She closed her eyes, trying not to cry, but she couldn't stop the tears. Blaze nudged her arm and tried to speak. All he could manage was a sad squeak. Tinker Bell put her hand on him. "I'm sorry, Blaze. It's not your fault. It's mine. All mine."

Blaze laid his head on her knee like a puppy. Tink was touched by his ability to forgive so quickly. Why couldn't everybody be like Blaze? Why couldn't she? Why couldn't Terence? She missed her friend so much. "I wish Terence were here," she said out loud. "I wish we were still friends."

She gazed at the mirror. There was no magic left

in it now. Only the reflection of her own heartbroken face. One of her tears fell onto the glass.

Suddenly, Tink heard Terence's voice. "We *are* friends, Tink."

Tink held up the mirror, her tear cutting a track through the dust and grime. She could just barely make out the shape of another face in the reflection. Terence's face. She drew in her breath. "Terence," she said to the mirror. "I am so sorry."

"I forgive you," Terence said gently.

"I miss you so much," Tink sadly told the face in the glass.

"I miss you, too. But Tink, why didn't you tell me about the moonstone?"

"I didn't want anyone to know. I didn't think I needed any help. Terence, I was wrong. I wish you were here."

"I am here," the reflection told her.

"I know you are," Tink said. "But I mean really here. With me."

"I am really here with you."

"No. I mean right next to me."

"Tink," the reflection said. "I'm standing right behind you. You're looking at me in the mirror."

Tink turned, and there he was. Right there. Right beside her. Just like he said. She threw her arms around him. "Terence! I am so sorry."

Terence hugged her back. "I'm sorry, too. You were under a lot of pressure and—"

Blaze flew over and tried to squeeze between them.

"Hey! Who's this?" Terence asked.

Tinker Bell stood back so that Blaze could get his share of hugs. "This is Blaze. He's been a big help in some tough spots."

"It's a pleasure to meet you," Terence said to Blaze.

"How did you find me?" Tink asked.

"I flew all night and all day over the sea—it's a good thing you left that trail of pots and pans across Never Land," Terence explained. "Then, just when I was going to run out of pixie dust, I stumbled into that flying machine of yours. That thing is awesome. I only had a pinch of dust left, but it got me all the way here."

"You found my balloon? But where did you get the dust to make it this far?"

"I . . . uh . . . 'borrowed' a little extra."

"You broke the rules for me?"

"I knew you needed my help."

Tink was about to throw her arms around him one more time, when she saw something emerging from the shadows. "Terence. Look!"

A rat appeared. Then another. Soon Tink and Terence were surrounded by a pack of rats. And they looked hungry.

The fairies didn't lose any time. Terence grabbed the satchel with the moonstone fragments. Tink pulled the compass needle from the wall and stuck it in her belt.

Only one thing left to do now . . .

RUN!

Chapter Fourteen

Tinker Bell and Terence took off as fast as they could. Blaze flew behind, trying to provide cover. He dive-bombed the rats, using his loudest buzz and brightest light to distract and confuse them.

More rats came pouring out of every dark hole and crack in the ship.

Terence grabbed Tinker Bell's hand and pulled her along through the disintegrating grandeur of the rotting ship. They ran over a globe, slid across the curved surface, and landed on a grand piano, which let out an ominous and out-of-tune chord of protest. "Hold on," Terence said. He grabbed a tattered curtain ribbon with one hand and wrapped his other arm around Tink's waist. They swung across the room. Halfway across, the ribbon snapped.

They plummeted, landing on a stack of old dinner plates. The stack teetered for a moment, then began to slide across the table.

Tinker Bell and Terence held out their arms for balance as they rode one of the plates like a sled. They made a graceful leap to safety just before the plate hit a banister and shattered into pieces.

Terence grinned. "That was kind of fun."

The fun didn't last long, though. More rats—an ocean of rats—came rushing at them. Terence pointed toward a crevice in the ship's wall. "There's our way out."

Tink and Terence tried to squeeze through, but the crevice was too tight. They would have to pry away one of the boards. They tugged at one of the planks with all their might. It wouldn't budge.

"Terence, buy me some time," Tinker Bell said as she pulled the needle from her belt and tossed it to him. He turned, wielding the needle like a sword as the rats closed in. "Back!" he yelled, whisking the needle back and forth to hold them at bay. "Back!"

Tinker Bell and Blaze leaped behind a pile of debris for cover. Suddenly, Tink had an idea. Rummaging through her satchel, she found the mirror and some dirty cobwebs. A few deft movements later, she was ready.

She peered over the bank of debris and saw one of the rats knock the needle from Terence's hand. The rat lunged. Terence dodged just in time. But when he turned, he was greeted by a group of rats with their teeth bared. They were beginning to close in when, suddenly, their eyes were distracted by something.

The rodents fell back, squeaking in fear. The huge shadow of a monster loomed on the wall. A bone-chilling growl echoed through the ship. The shadow began to move and grew even larger.

That was it for the rats. They turned and ran, climbing over one another in panic. Their shrieks and squeaks gradually faded as they disappeared into the most distant reaches of the hull.

"Are they gone?" Tinker Bell whispered.

Terence stood very still and listened to be sure. "Yeah! Let's go."

Tinker Bell took one last look around before putting her props away. The monster had been an illusion created by the mirror, the cobwebs, and Blaze's clever lighting.

And the growl had been Blaze, using Tink's folded hat as a megaphone. He was still growling away and having a wonderful time. Tink snatched her hat back and the menacing sounds returned to Blaze's customary squeak. "Come here, you vicious monster!" She grabbed the mischievous firefly and gave him a big hug. Blaze blinked happily.

Tinker Bell grinned at her companions. The three of them were a good team. Now all they had to do was get back to Pixie Hollow.

That and one or two other things—like fixing the scepter and figuring out what to do about the moonstone. But at least now she wasn't trying to do all those things by herself.

Chapter Fifteen

Terence had left the balloon tied to the mast of the pirate ship. Very carefully, the three friends climbed the rotten rigging and scrambled into the balloon's basket. "How are we going to fly this thing?" Terence muttered, untying the ropes. "I used the last of my dust getting it this far."

Tinker Bell rummaged around in the bottom of the basket. "With any luck, my pixie dust bag should be around here somewhere. Aha!" She held up her little velvet bag and tossed it to Terence. "Here. Is it enough?"

He untied the strings and looked inside. "It's enough," he confirmed. "Anchors up."

Tink saluted. "Aye, aye, Captain." Blaze mimicked her salute.

"Just a little bit of pixie dust up front will get this baby going." Terence rubbed some dust on the bow of the balloon. "There, that should do the trick."

The bow began to glow. Then it lurched into the air as if it were excited to be released from its tether. Terence fell back against the rudder and grabbed it, straightening their course.

Soon they were sailing over the water, on their way back to Pixie Hollow.

On and on they flew, making good time the whole way. By sunset, they were almost there.

But Tink's relief at escaping the rats had turned to apprehension over what would happen when she got back home. Her friends seemed to sense the change in her mood. "Are you okay?" Terence asked. Blaze hovered with concern.

"What's going to happen when we get back?" Tink asked. She picked up the bag that held the moonstone fragments and shook it sadly. "Would you happen to have an extra moonstone?"

Terence's face grew serious. He picked up a bag from the floor of the balloon. "I don't know if it will help, but I brought this."

Tink opened the bag. "My scepter!" She took out one of the broken pieces of the scepter and examined it next to a tiny shard of moonstone. Was there any way to repair them? Any way at all?

Terence leaned over her shoulder, and Blaze flew in close so he could see. The light from his tail bounced off the mirror and refracted through the shard. Streams of brilliant blue light shot out in every direction.

"Terence!"

Terence stepped back. "Oh, yeah. Sorry. I know you need your space."

"It's not that," she said eagerly. "I have an idea. And I can't do it without you. Will you help me?"

Terence's face broke into a wide smile. Those were just the words he had been waiting to hear. "Sure."

Tinker Bell positioned Blaze so that he could cast enough light for her to work. Terence gathered up everything in the balloon that could possibly be used as a tool. And the three of them buckled down to do their task. The future of Pixie Hollow depended on them.

That night, as their balloon flew steadily toward Pixie Hollow, Tinker Bell and Terence hammered, tapped, rapped, twisted, and tweaked, determined to repair the damage, not just to the scepter, but also to their friendship. They politely and eagerly exchanged and accepted advice from each other. It wasn't long before they were finishing each other's sentences and anticipating each other's next move— just like in the old days.

"If I turn this, then this can go in here," Tink said.

"Wait a second . . . do you think this would work?" Terence asked.

"Yes. Yes."

"Okay. Now set it at a thirty-degree angle so that the reflective qualities of the moonstone—"

"—are magnified in relation to the moonbeam rays. You're a genius!" Tink said. Little by little, the pieces began to fit together. She pressed a shard into the scepter's handle. "I've almost got it. I just need—"

"A sharp thingy," Terence offered. He held out the compass needle. Tink smiled gratefully and took it from him. Yes. That was exactly what she needed. Too bad she had been too stubborn to realize it before.

As night fell, Blaze buzzed brighter, and the blue moon rose into the sky.

Back in Pixie Hollow, the fairies were gathering in the forest for the Autumn Revelry. Fairy Mary was in a state of panic. Where was Tinker Bell? *Where?* The ceremony was starting. The blue moon was rising. The music fairies were already sounding the fanfare on their flower trumpets, but Tinker Bell was nowhere to be seen.

Fairy Mary wrung her hands and paced, counting frantically to calm herself. She'd been counting for a long time and was way past ten. "One thousand four hundred and ninety-two . . . one thousand four hundred and ninety-three . . . one thousand four hundred and ninety-four . . ."

Bobble and Clank followed her back and forth, trying to soothe her. "Now, now," Bobble clucked.

"It's all right," Clank crooned. "Tink will be here any second now."

Fairy Mary watched Queen Clarion and the Minister of Autumn proceed to the stage.

Fairy Gary and the other dust-keepers followed. They carried huge cauldrons to catch the blue pixie dust. Fairy Gary's cauldron was the largest. "It's a bit heavier than I remember," he said, placing it on top of a holder with a grunt.

Fairy Mary groaned and slumped to the ground. "The blue harvest moon is high. The moonbeams are almost at their mark. This is a disaster." Clank and Bobble hoisted her back up and made more soothing noises—but nothing they could say would help.

The Minister of Autumn stuck his head backstage and hissed, "Fairy Mary! Where is Tinker Bell?"

"I don't know!" Fairy Mary wailed.

The Minister of Autumn's brows shot up and his eyes bulged. "You . . . you . . . *don't know?*"

Now Queen Clarion had stepped backstage. "Fairy Mary, Minister of Autumn. Is anything the matter?"

"Yes, Your Highness," said the Minister of Autumn.

"No, Your Highness," Fairy Mary said at the exact same time.

Queen Clarion clasped her hands together and narrowed her eyes. "Where is Tinker Bell?" she asked.

Fairy Mary's head began to spin. This was terrible. This was awful. So awful she could hardly get the words out. "Um . . . well . . . uh . . . we've been . . . uh . . ."

Fairy Mary cast her eyes upward so she wouldn't have to meet Queen Clarion's stern gaze. And to her utter amazement, she saw a huge balloon sweeping down with Tink and Terence hanging from the rigging.

"There she is," Fairy Mary said with a sigh of relief so deep, she almost fell over again.

"Hello!" Tinker Bell called out, waving.

By now, all the fairies who had gathered for the revelry had spotted the balloon. A roar of applause filled the forest. Fairy Mary and the queen watched as the balloon settled on some tree branches. Tink and Terence stepped out, followed by Blaze.

"I made it," Tinker Bell said happily.

"Now, *that's* an entrance!" Queen Clarion said. A smile lurked at the corners of her mouth.

"Right in the nick of time," Bobble said approvingly.

The fairies continued to cheer as Tinker Bell approached the queen, dropping down on one knee. "Your Highness," she said respectfully.

Queen Clarion gestured to the fairies to be quiet. When the forest was silent, she spoke. "Tinker Bell. At the beginning of the season you were entrusted with a great responsibility. Where is the Autumn Scepter?"

Fairy Mary squeezed her fists so hard, she could feel her nails digging into her palms. Had Tinker Bell succeeded?

Tinker Bell lifted her head, and her large eyes were full of apology. "There were some . . . uhhhh . . . complications."

Fairy Mary felt the color drain from her face. Queen Clarion turned to look at her, as if to ask whether she knew anything about this. Fairy Mary gave a tiny shake of her head.

"But it's ready now, Your Highness." Tink turned, and Terence handed her something wrapped in a leaf.

Queen Clarion led Tinker Bell to the stage. "This way, Tinker Bell."

Tink placed the shrouded scepter in a special holder in the middle of the stage. "Fairies of Pixie Hollow, I present . . . the Autumn Scepter."

Tink whipped off the leaf, and Fairy Mary felt her eyes bulge and her heart stop.

If *that* was a scepter, then Fairy Mary was a june bug. It didn't look like a scepter at all. It looked like an old hand mirror with bits of gold and scepter shards glued all around it. Artistic, and well . . . beautiful, in a Tinker Bell kind of way. But where was the orderly, geometric design Tinker Bell had shown them? *And where was the moonstone?*

Fairy Mary peered more closely and realized that the moonstone was in pieces. Once again, her head began to swim. This was a tragedy. A huge disaster.

The one and only moonstone was broken!

Fairy Mary clenched and unclenched her hands and began to count as if her life depended on it. Actually, as if *Tinker Bell's* life depended on it. Because if Fairy Mary ever got her hands around Tinker Bell's neck . . . "One thousand four hundred and ninety—"

But before Fairy Mary could get the word *five* out of her mouth, the world went black and she fainted.

Chapter Sixteen

Tinker Bell saw Fairy Mary collapse. "No. No. No. Don't worry, Fairy Mary. It's okay. Just wait." Tink sounded confident, but inside, she was quaking. *Will it work? Will it really work?*

Fairy Mary woke up, but she didn't look happy.

Terence stared up at the moon. "Come on. Come on . . . ," he urged.

"Please work," Tinker Bell whispered. "Please."

Blaze flew in circles and crossed his antennae.

As all the fairies watched, holding their breath, the moon moved into its final position. Its rays touched the scepter and—*WHOOSH!*—the result was spectacular.

Thousands of beams reflected off the fragments. Brilliant blue rays went streaking into the crowd, followed by a light shower of blue pixie dust raining from the sky.

A roar of approval shook the forest. The fairies lifted their hands to catch the dust as it fell. At first, it was just a flurry. Then it turned into a dust fall; then a blizzard. The wonderful, magical blue pixie dust piled around them in deep drifts.

The Minister of Autumn and Queen Clarion were awestruck. "Your Majesty," said the Minister, "I've never seen this much blue pixie dust before!"

"Indeed" was all Queen Clarion seemed to be able to say.

Fairy Mary was too happy and relieved to speak. Fairy Gary stood on a pile of dust that reached all the way to his chest. "It's at least a million smidges. Maybe more."

Silvermist flew in giddy circles. "This is amazing!" she exclaimed, almost out of breath.

Fawn created snow angels in the dust. "Wooo-hooo!"

"Come on, girls!" Rosetta shouted. "It's show-time."

Queen Clarion held up her hands and called them to order. "Fairies of Pixie Hollow, we have celebrated this revelry without interruption for centuries. Tonight, I believe, is our finest revelry ever—thanks to one special fairy, Tinker Bell."

Tinker Bell pulled Terence close beside her and pointed at him, trying to get Queen Clarion's attention.

Queen Clarion nodded. "Oh . . . yes . . . and her friend Terence."

Blaze circled Tink and Terence close beside her, blinking and buzzing.

"And . . . her *new* friend," Queen Clarion added, unsure what to call the bright bug.

"Blaze," Tinker Bell whispered.

"Blaze," Queen Clarion told the fairies. "We owe them all our thanks!"

The fairies applauded and cheered. Fairy Mary came and gave Tink a hug. "I'm so proud of you," she said.

"Thank you, Fairy Mary," Tinker Bell responded.

"What made you think of breaking the moonstone into all those tiny pieces?" Fairy Mary asked. "Genius."

Tinker Bell really didn't want to lie, but she didn't want to tell the truth, either. Luckily, she didn't have to answer the question, because the Minister of Autumn approached her, holding the scepter. He solemnly handed it to her. "On your lead, my dear." Then he turned toward the crowd. "All right, everyone. To the Pixie Dust Tree!"

Proudly, Tinker Bell raised the scepter and began to lead the procession.

"That's our cue," Fawn told the other fairies. She blew a whistle, and the beautiful special effects began.

The sky turned bright yellow as the twenty-one-butterfly salute successfully launched into the air.

Silvermist's tadpoles blew bubbles that danced and sparkled overhead.

Clank joyfully ran to his fireworks launcher and let 'er rip.

KABOOM!

The fireworks split the contraption in two, but it

didn't matter—it still managed to hurl fireworks into the sky. Sparkling, sizzling patterns in every color streaked this way and that, reflecting off each happy face in Pixie Hollow.

"It worked, Bobble! It worked!" Clank hollered happily. To celebrate, he sprinkled a bit of the blue pixie dust on Cheese the mouse.

Cheese took to the air, flying along with everyone else as they soared over the waterfall, over the meadows, and took their place on the Pixie Dust Tree, where Lyria was waiting.

Tinker Bell and Terence stood in a place of honor and held up the scepter together. Blaze circled happily, proud to be a part of this momentous occasion.

Fairy Gary and the other dust-keepers carried in the cauldrons full of blue dust. They poured the precious magic into the well of the tree while Lyria recited the poem she had prepared to commemorate the miracle of autumn—a miracle that couldn't have taken place if not for all the fairies in Pixie Hollow.

The greatest treasures are not gold,
Nor jewels, nor works of art.
They cannot be held in your hands—
They're held within your heart.
For worldly things will fade away
As seasons come and go.
But the treasure of true friendship
Will never lose its glow.